MID RIVERS REVIEW

2014

St. Charles Community College
Cottleville, Missouri

VOLUME XV

Editor	Virginia Guneyli
Associate Editor	Christina Gant
Art Editor	Kathleen Sanker
Readers	Lindsay Brand
	Jacqueline Gray
	Bryonie Carter
Cover Photo	Brian D. Smith
Layout Design	Stephen Schuknecht

Mid Rivers Review is published annually by the English Department at St. Charles Community College. Views expressed here do not necessarily reflect those of the college or the editor.

Copyright © 2014 by St. Charles Community College. Rights revert to authors upon publication.

We invite submissions of original poetry, short fiction, prose and visual art. For full submission guidelines visit our website: www.stchas.edu/midriversreview. Address correspondence to Editor, English Dept., HUM 203 St. Charles Community College, 4601 Mid Rivers Mall Dr., Cottleville, MO 63376.

Printed in the United States by Formax Printing Solutions. ISBN 978-0-9825372-4-4

FOR SCOTTIE AND JACQUELINE

FROM THE EDITOR

As Brian Smith's stunning cover photo suggests, there is much to discover in this issue of *Mid Rivers Review*. Jacqueline Gray, previous editor, worked on it through the depths of winter when we all tend to muse "about spring and whether or not it still exists," as Kasey Perkins does in her poem, "The First Storm of February." Sometime between the "first blooms of spring, pollen lightly dusting cars," of which Amber Scholl writes and the "blooming vibrance" of summer, captured in Erin Petty's eponymous photo, Jacqueline gave me some of the words and images of the artists whose work comprises this issue. And now, with the hint of the "jewel-tipped trees" of autumn that Julie Varwig celebrates, we have finished. We desire this *Mid Rivers Review* to persist and, as Percy Bysshe Shelley writes, " quicken a new birth…" and spread ideas and "words among Mankind."

This is the sixth year we have awarded a deserving writer and contributor with the Jim Haba Poetry Award. Haba, a poet and leader, directed the Geraldine R. Dodge Poetry Festival for 22 years. His work has changed the lives of countless poets and lovers of poetry. This year, we are honoring a young poet on the rise, Harleigh Heck. She masters and refines her work to convey her raw spirit; she inserts dashing lines of wit and mirth into poetry that explores the most difficult of life's challenges.

We are immensely grateful to the Board of Directors, faculty, administration, and staff of St. Charles Community College for their support of *Mid Rivers Review*. We are indebted to our colleagues, Kathleen Sanker and Alison Ouellette-Kirby, for guiding the artists and advising the editors.

Thanks to Christy Gant for her encouragement and help. And Lindsay Brand—new mother, professor, wife, daughter, and friend —somehow found time to read and edit this issue multiple times. She also resisted the urge to screen my calls when I phoned her to ask for even more help and time.

Stephen Schuknecht, who is a former student of both Kathleen Sanker's and mine and a graduate of St. Charles Community College, worked tirelessly and lovingly to design and typeset something beautiful for readers to hold in their hands or read on their devices. Stephen is unfailingly detailed, committed and kind. He often worked until 2 am. Emails are time-stamped, so I know the truth, despite his repeated assurances that he was sleeping and eating healthfully during this arduous process. He wasn't.

I would also like to thank my beloved family—Bulent, Nuri, and Nora—for being understanding when I got home late and sometimes didn't hear them because I was engrossed in reading, thinking, or discussing *Mid Rivers Review*.

Most of all, I would like to thank all the contributors. This book is by them and for them, and it always has been.

Finally, I offer thanks to and for Scottie Priesmeyer and Jacqueline Gray. For everything they have created with us and for us through the years, we are grateful, and we dedicate this issue to you.

Scottie retired last May. She served the English department, the community, and the college for sixteen years, and she was once an editor of this journal. It was in Scottie's former office that I did most of the work on this issue, and I felt her good energy each day. All of us did.

Jacqueline Gray stepped down as editor last summer, not before lovingly and gracefully helping me transition into that position. One of her most admirable qualities is that she explains things in a way that I (and most anyone) can understand. While working with her as the Co-Assistant Editor last year, we met often in her office to read and talk about the issue. I frequently fixated on an old mining pick she propped against a stack of books on a shelf. I asked her for the story, for I knew there was one. She told me that her great-grandfather, Joseph Blackwood Gray (a man as strong as his name), mined with it in Chestnut Hill Mine, Mercer County, Pennsylvania, in the 1880s. That pick, as well as Harleigh Heck's

poem, "Writing for a Miner," elicit a central metaphor in Seamus Heaney's, "Digging":

"Between my finger and my thumb, the squat pen rests. I'll dig with it."

In these pages, you will find that much digging has been done.

Sincerely,
Virginia Guneyli, Editor

INTRODUCTION

"I don't read a lot of poetry, but what really shocked me the most about your work was that you're such a sweet person." That was the very first thing the fiction writer Mary Troy had to say about my book this year. Whatever good or bad this may say regarding me as a person aside, I couldn't help but laugh at this particular critique. It is one of the single greatest aspects of poetry: the ability to become anything.

The first poem I read for this volume of the *Mid Rivers Review* was Kristen Garcia's "Queer," and it embodies this idea. For all but its last line, the poem seems to be the back-and-forth morning navigation of a man and a woman getting ready to face their day. They get dressed, eat breakfast, pack lunch - and finally "he" steps into the bathroom to look in the mirror, "only to see Her peering back." Surprise! This poem is not what it seemed to be on the surface, and only countless re-readings allow us to get all of Garcia's little hints and nuances in this seemingly simple twelve line poem. Just a few weeks ago, I took a straw poll in my composition class at SCC: does Sharon Olds think you should be in love in order to have sex? Most of my students said no. Then we spent about forty five minutes re-examining Olds' "Sex Without Love," and all the ways you could mean "how do they do it." Now we think you need love for sex, but most of us aren't really sure anymore. And that's poetry for you.

The best writers are full of these little dual meanings and contradictions. Fault a poet for contradictions, and he may well shout Whitman's, "I am large,

I contain multitudes!" just because he can. It's how Jordan Starkey, who has two poems in this edition, can spend his time brooding about the inevitability of death and how immortality is a farce—and yet spend all his waking free time writing love sonnets to his wife. It's how Diana Nash can make sense of the junk drawer in her brain, as she does in the poem "Junk."

It's how Harleigh Heck can show us a girl in a homespun jacket with the loving fire to throw it to safety before she dives into a fight to protect that very jacket. Heck asks, "let me be, let me mine / let me mine my diamonds." That's what all writers do—sift through the brain for the simplest, yet most complex, most faceted gems so that we may bring them to light and life.

Towards the end of this collection, Lindsay Brand writes in "Cerulean Blue Period" that "it's the simple pleasures of life that really make life meaningful and shit. Then they tell me to get a job in an office." Well, I have a job that comes with an office, and I can tell you this: a writer can make meaning of anything, and those connections are one of life's greatest pleasures. They can also make meaning anywhere—including the Office. And that's what the writers in this volume of *Mid Rivers Review* do.

Naomi Shihab Nye once said that "we're all poets when we're little...some of us just like to keep up the habit." Thankfully, everyone in this edition has done just that.

-Kasey Perkins

POETRY AND SHORT PROSE

Harleigh Heck
2014 Haba Award Winner
Writing For a Miner (Haba Award Winner) **13**
Fight with Honor **14**
Hands Up **14**
Death of a Star **15**
So Do Not Offer **16**
Sweet Daphne **17**

Kristen Garcia
Queer **18**
Spirit **18**

Lauren Pearson
Midnight Heartbeat **20**
Tips For Finding A Subway Seat **21**
Snapshots Of Puffy Eyes **23**

Dana Delibovi
Aurora **24**
Swamp Grass **25**
First Divorced Winter at the Beach **27**

Daron Kappauff
Words That Have No Meaning (But Burn Just As Well) **28**

Hali Pace
Face It **30**
Growing Up With My Dad **33**

Sara Welch
The Holocene **34**

Lacey Garland
What Do You Think of This Girl **37**
Pound Cake **37**

Amber Scholl
The Map **38**
Seasons **43**
Journey **44**
The Nature of Beauty **45**
Blind Silence (To Liz Sheck) **47**

Courtney Allen
The Quiet **48**
Confident **49**

Julie E. Varwig
Jewel-Tipped Trees and a Kiss **50**
As the River **53**
The Front Yard Lies **54**

Mary Kane
The Three Wishes **57**

Cameron Beck	*Earthien Sonnet* **58** *Nora the Redeemer* **60**
Emily McGuire	*Astronomy* **61**
Tyra Bowman	*Fleur* **63** *Mulatto* **64**
Sabrina Teeple	*Cannibal* **65** *DIY Psych* **67**
Megan Zehnder	*Ode to a Tree* **68** *The Wife* **71**
Miriam Hannibal	*Cast* **72** *My Last Lullaby* **72**
Jordan Starkey	*Serenade Betrayed* **74** *Dignity Digested* **74**
Lindsay Brand	*Cerulean Blue Period* **76** *On Rabbits* **77**
Dianna Nash	*Junk* **79** *NCLB* **80**
Shamgaud Shuttlesworth	*Military Poetrie* **82**
Mary Horner	*Cacophony* **85** *Memory Lame* **86**
Kasey Perkins	*The Metatarsal Galaxy* **87** *Mississippi Night* **88** *Inheritance* **89** *The First Storm of February* **90**
Kim Lee Seagull	*The Canadian Snowbird* **93**
Haley McGrotty	*The First Time* **94**
Amber Dunlap	*The Mausoleum* **97**

PHOTOGRAPHY AND ILLUSTRATION

Kathleen Beardsell — *Oscar* **29**
Giant Washbowl **51**
Baby Birds **55**
Mourier **96**

Cameron Beck — *Earth* **59**

Hannah Clark — *Found My Marbles* **78**

Debra Crank-Lewis — *Riverbed On A Distant World* **35**
Things Half-Seen **46**
Springtime on the Mississippi **52**

Kayla Czajkowski — *Hanging on the Line* **70**
Little Lamb **73**
Deer Creek **91**
Winter's Perch **92**

Tim Hahn — *Studio View* **83**

Crystal Ianelli — *City Girl* **36**
Blowing in the Wind **69**

Yvonne Koch — *Reach* **49**

Jessica Luebbert — *Walk with a Mural* **41**

Alison Ouellette-Kirby — *Joseph Blackwood Gray: A Miner's Pick* **12**

Erin Petty — *River's Edge* **25**
Interwoven Paths **26**
Blooming Vibrance **62**

Warren Rich — *Lobby Boxer* **84**

Henry Salazar — *Parallelism* **86**

Sarah Salveggio — *Three-Dimensions* **16**

Brian Smith — *Green Door* **Cover Photo**

April Stout — *Slayer of the Dragon* **32**

Sabrina Teeple   *In the Basement* **66**

Russell Ward   *Track Star* **77**

Julie Westrich   *Pieces of Myself* **19**
Idea of Peace in a Fish Tank **95**

Sue Wolf   *Untitled* **22**
Misery **42**
Jake Heels **56**
Alex **61**

Given Zane   *Potted Meat* **75**

Joseph Blackwood Gray: A Miner's Pick | Alison Ouellette-Kirby

HARLEIGH HECK

Writing for a Miner

I have thrown
the dirt of exasperation
over my shoulder
into a pile that has grown.
I am the only miner in creation
in this cave of gems and boulders.
My light can only show
so much at one time
in its limited amount of seconds
before the bulb burns its last glow.
So let me be, let me mine,
let me find my diamonds.

RECIPIENT
OF THE 2014
JAMES HABA
POETRY AWARD

HARLEIGH HECK

Fight with Honor

When my mother was young,
she wore a homemade coat,
and after seeing all the pride
that my grandmother put into it,
she felt the taunts of others,
but she was still so proud of the fine cloth,
that whenever she would fight,
she took her coat off.

Hands Up

You're surrounded by treasures,
we've received together,
from journeys to wherever we pleased,
You're surrounded by photos,
of family long since gone,
wondering why you are here.
You're surrounded by sadness,
from a lack of time,
spent with me.

Death of a Star

Spinning in the black abyss,
my warmth,
I share around me,
They come and go,
rotation,
I grow old,
I've worn for many a year,
Now I no longer last,
Expanding—Growing—Swelling,
my red skin corrupts all,
engulfing the revolutionaries,
that surround me,
few are left,
I reach for those,
that I did not harm,
but they—as I—have changed,
Slowly I wither,
away.
Death becomes me.
But I do not cease,
reborn again am I,
a dwarf—
of my former self,
though I can still outshine,
any star in the night—
sky.

HARLEIGH HECK

So Do Not Offer

I do not wish to eat,
in your presence.
For I am not the squirrel,
who eats moldy feed.
I do not wish to play,
in your presence.
For I am not the fish,
who swims in a puddle.
I do not wish to love,
in your presence.
For I am not the soldier,
who dies in the field.

Three-Dimensions | Sarah Salveggio

Sweet Daphne

I sing unto you,
lullabies of Loretta Lynn,
and watch you drift into dreams,
while thinking of him.
You wake me early,
for a tad of fresh air,
right after I've fallen to sleep,
I close the door and you linger there.
You stare at my plate full of food,
and wonder why you look different than me,
why we drop food bits if only in the mood.
Yet you hate the diet we give you.
"Please do not leave,"
"Come with me to play,"
"I love you,"
This is what you say.
I'll miss you when you're gone,
for your memory will loom,
and I'm already crying,
as your tail slips through the door and
my friend leaves the room.

KRISTEN GARCIA

Queer

She awakes at eight in the morning
He swings his legs over the side of the bed
She goes and makes her breakfast tea
He picks out something to wear
She puts on a cute dress
He does up the laces of his boots
She gets the tea into her mug
He packs an easy lunch
She gets on her jewelry
He finally stumbles in the bathroom
And looks at the mirror
Only to see Her peering back

Spirit

Flowers grew from her eyes
And sprouts from her lips
Her hair housed weeds
And her body a field
She spoke rivers
And sang mountains
She danced valleys
And sighed clouds
Her light brought joy
And her dark brought comfort
Her wind changed the land
And her rain gave it purpose.

Pieces of Myself | Julie Westrich

LAUREN PEARSON

Midnight Heartbeat

At night I place my hand over my heart.
Feeling for the beat that means I'm still alive.
Still here. Still breathing. Still worth it.

I can remember the day you brought me flowers.
You showed up, shirt pressed, with that same sad smile.
I didn't want to tell you the truth.
That my lips had already known another man,
That my finger tips burned at the thought of his skin.
So instead I told you that I only saw you as a friend,
Despite the weeks of rough sex and stolen time together.
After everything, how could I admit that you were so much more?

I'd already proven that you were clearly not enough.
Tonight I'll place my hand over my heart with tears in my eyes.
Praying that for once I'll be able to believe its beat means
I'm still alive.

Tips For Finding A Subway Seat

When the girl with sunken eyes and white lips mutters
to herself on the subway, remind her that there are plenty of things
to worry about, but for her, losing weight isn't one of them.

When she gets off at your stop, invite her for coffee.
Even if her eyes are throwing daggers at you, and even if every
instinct in a normal person would be yelling that her track marks
are just that, track marks, and for all you know she might just shove
a letter opener into your stomach for the contents of your pockets.
A few bucks for another spoonful of hell.

Lace your fingers in hers after she reluctantly agrees,
and without missing a beat, talk about how no girl should pass up
free coffee or free alcohol. After all, there is the economy to think about.

Gossip to her about people you pass on the street, and when she settles into
her signature silence, tell her about how you love to make up life stories for the
people you see outside your apartment window, and how you've never
admitted that to anyone else.

When she leaves, after a warm vanilla latte and two cinnamon bagels,
tell her that you should do this again sometime, and make plans to
meet her again next week.

When next week rolls around, don't be surprised to see your
alley rat friend missing. Instead, smile and think about all the important
reasons she couldn't make it. Like staying in to finish a term paper
for law school, or picking up an extra shift at the local volunteer hospital.

Then turn to the little boy next to you, scared, dirty,
and without parents, and offer to walk him to the local church center.
Because these days, no one should have to feel alone.

Untitled | Sue Wolf

LAUREN PEARSON

Snapshots Of Puffy Eyes

Yesterday I sat on your porch, and drew pink chalk hearts
around your doormat. You asked me if I wanted sweet tea
and I said yes, though all I really wanted was your lips
against my ear. Whispering how much you missed the smell
of my perfume on your pillow.

And sometimes I take snapshot of my face when I cry.
I mail them to you in a grey envelope and on the back of
every one I write down confessions about what animals
I'd run over in the road that day, and how they all made
the same loud thump under my wheels, no matter how
hard I pushed on the gas pedal, or how much
I turned up the stereo.

Occasionally you bring the pictures back to me, telling me
everything you know about radio waves, road kill, and how
they relate to the tread on my tires. You tell me things I won't
ever need to know, but will never be able to forget no matter
how many times I try to burn the memories of you
from my frontal lobe.

I guess that's another reason why I love you.
Because no one's ever told me how they make the
colors in my favorite fourth of July fireworks.

DANA DELIBOVI

Aurora

In the hour of the birds,
in the hour of purple air,
every second is a fresh start.

Before dreamers surrender to facts,
Before planners founder in entropy,
Before workers in fluorescent rooms
get walled off from the dogwoods,
the world is shimmering around them all.

To reach through morning light
toward a spider straggling to his hole,
or to listen with the whole ear
as a cardinal pipes on the swing-set,
is to open a small, early window
that shuts on the fingers later in the day.

River's Edge | Erin Petty

The Swamp Grass

At the rim of the salt marsh, where
            Nor'easters blow the waters high,
                      the swamp grass mourned.
The six-foot fronds, strong enough
            only for a goldfinch, rustled
                      with the sighs of great girls
grieving oceanic loss: uprooted stands
            of wild roses, drowned muskrats,
                      topsoil claimed by tidal floods.
Like murmuring daughters at a wake,
            each frond forced its hollow self
                      to choke any strident sound.

Interwoven Paths | Erin Petty

DANA DELIBOVI

First Divorced Winter at the Beach

1
BMW
parked by the snowy playground
over a dead eel.

2
I walk the sand. Gulls
skim water on ice-willed wings.
Far off, a snowplow groans.

3
Orange firethorn fruits
and the blue afternoon make
a fool out of me.

4
The mansion's garden
hangs over the sea wall—I steal
juniper berries.

5
Birches drop catkins.
This his Beamer, etched with frost?
A tern pounds water.

6
Bits of blue sea-glass
peek through slush, near the
plywood-boarded summerhouse.

7
January likes
grubby ropes of kelp. I like
some guy I don't know.

8
Waving fragmites,
sunset water, a wooden sign:
Bluewater Hill. Keep Out.

9
Moon at dusk. A glove
lies lost on the snowy beach,
nosed by a black dog.

10
I'm back at his car.
The wind lifts up cold ripples
On the inlet's skin.

DARON KAPPAUFF

Words That Have No Meaning (But Burn Just as Well)

Words read me—spell out my name and release
my past to the wind—
     through trees, time, and your hair -
events move unhindered from you.

Words read me—place my tomorrows in the ground,
nurture their dying roots,
their vapid days that bare no grace—
the contour of fire left from your absence.

Words read me—spew their vowels
in my face and over the lives of those
     whose lives spark against mine -
on the sheets, the pillow and all across the scene of framed
remorse.

Words read me—pronounce judgment, and rejoice
     in the glow of our last goodbye—
     in the solitude
of freedom that bares no shame, and price that hides no
smile.

Words write me -
     fill in the blanks,
and discard a tear for the fading night.

Oscar | Kathleen Beardsell

HALI PACE

Face It

My grandfather couldn't face it.
Couldn't look us in the eye.
The things he saw
The things he did
They sat ever present in his eyes.
The eyes that matched the color of my brothers
so perfectly.
We would plant saplings in his yard
He'd dig the hole, while I held the trees
I'd watch him
Bent over, back facing the sun.
He tore at the ground angrily
Like an answer lay under the roots
of the bright green grass.
Every once in awhile he'd stop
He'd wipe his hands on an old mechanic's rag
I'd watch as he scrubbed at his nails
Like he was wiping away the blood of those
he couldn't protect.
I hated to watch him fidget with things
Eyes pleading with them to cooperate
The handle on his screwdriver
The same green as his old beret
I wonder how often his eyes had looked like that.
This past summer we went to the river
I sat with my grandfather on the bank
He showed me how to find unpolished garnets
Hidden among the jagged rocks.
We barely spoke
But that day was different

He wanted to know me
Maybe as deeply as I wanted to know him.
His pride rose with every garnet I found
Soaring
Airborne like the Ranger he once was.
Then he would look up at us
A smile in his eyes that didn't reach his lips
His brothers, sons, grandchildren, and I
My grandfather couldn't face it
But I don't think he ever had regret
Our family always knew he was a hero
A man beyond words
So maybe he never spoke of it.
Never told us the tale we knew was there.
But seeing us all around him.
Standing behind him like we couldn't do before our birth
Maybe that's how my grandfather can face it.
And like the unpolished garnets he was so proud of
I knew under his plain, rough surface
A beautiful gem sat
Radiating like the brave hero I've always known he was.

Slayer of the Dragon | April Stout

HALI PACE

Growing Up With My Dad

My Daddy, My Daddy
Can build cities of blocks
Color within the lines
Make Barbies talk.
My Dad, My Dad
Can skateboard like me
He reads the books I read
Wants to retire to the sea
My Dad, My Dad
Walks the flea market stalls
Finds treasures in trash
Laughs whenever I fall...
My Father, My Father
A parent, a friend
A man above words
Whom I'll love till the end.

SARA WELCH

The Holocene

Like the roots of,
Barren trees, standing
Naked and anxious
Atop the earth
Eroded,
I lay drained, dried-up
And hollow.
And I,
I see the gaze,
Of our sun,
and in the blinding of her
arms outstretched,
prepare to be swallowed up,
by them.
But I,
Am omitted-
As the wealth of,
Warmth,
And vitamin,
Are distributed-
I lay shriveled still,
As all that
Surrounds me, tries,
To take,
Deep breaths,
After a long winters,
Coma.
Decaying, deep

Into the soils,
Of my own sorrows-
Holocene.
A victim of,
Myself mostly-
Still, the merciless mother,
Is of no relief,
Her breath biting,
With rigor at,
My frost bitten,
Cheeks.
She and I,
Alike,
Praying for my
Expiration.
To no avail.
My fingers nestled,
Just beneath the shallow,
Dirt I once nurtured,
Fed fat and plentiful,
Now frail, fragile and
Skinny
As if,
It weren't afraid,
At all, to
Die, or of what,
Awaits us after.

Riverbed On A Distant World | Debra Crank-Lewis

City Girl | Crystal Ianelli

LACEY GARLAND

What Do You Think of This Girl

Think her a Saint.........but she is a Sinner
think Satan weeps on her behalf,
He does not,
He laughs with sick pleasure,
at how close to corruption she is,
her curiosity consumes her.
Like the flame of a fire.........Burning,
Yearning for flesh,
and Love.
What she actually wants, you see,
is to jump the guy,
with the bedroom eyes,
sitting on the bench across the street.

Pound Cake

Put the flour in the sifter,
Sift the flour,
The absurd amount of butter,
In the mixer,
Add this...and that,
Eventually, she'd have a cake,
"Mama," I'd say,
"Can I lick the whisk?"
"Sure, baby."
My Grandmother made my life, with a Pound Cake.

AMBER SCHOLL

The Map

Mother and daughter turn together for one last
wistful look at the house, the closest thing to home either
of them has known in a while, for this chance to commit its
every nook and crevice and moment to memory.
The cracked driveway and siding that's crumbling in places.
The willow tree in the yard and flowers out front, the crisp
brown of impending death creeping over their petals. The
cement porch adorned with a mat not yet weathered or worn.

Melinda sighs, sinks into the soft faux leather of the
diver's seat, flicks on the headlights to break through the
gloom that has settled beneath a thick layer of billowing
black clouds. The bags are in the backseat, bulky and
bulging with all the evidence they can hold of the past. A
crumpled map carpets the passenger side floor; dark ink
arrows illustrate the wrinkled, imperfect paper with its
curved roads and untidy jotted notes. The path to one
location after the next has been traced, scratched out, and
redrawn with multiple detours.

"I thought you said he wouldn't be able to find us here.
You said we'd be here for my birthday."

Melinda spares the mirror another glance, counts
the bags in the backseat for the sixth time. She sighs,
"You don't have to be here to have a birthday.
It'll still happen wherever you are in the world."

"That's not the point. I thought—"
"I thought so, too." Melinda tries not to snap at her

daughter, but emotions crackle like the lightening overhead, too close to the surface. Jittery fingers fumble to find the right key, jam it into the ignition. Her knuckles are a white vice upon the steering wheel. "Look, I'm sorry. I don't know how he's done it, but he's found out where we've been staying. We don't have a choice. It can't—"

"—be helped," finishes Taylor, harshness evaporating in response to her mother's electric anxiety. "I know."

In its cozy shabbiness, its run-down hominess, the dwelling they are abandoning now is reminiscent of another, one long ago forgotten by Taylor, lost to those slippery childhood years that seem to always wriggle out of the reach of memory. But Melinda can still recall the sleepless nights and anxious days, terror and fury and finality in the form of curses and bruises to match. All the darkness masked by a quaint exterior.

But she'd thrown off the shackles when she'd tossed away the ring, that cold diamond restraint. The one precious outcome—the one part of those four long years of marriage that Melinda still treasures—sits with her arms crossed in the passenger seat, now committing to memory yet another home she has lost. More valuable by far than any ring, more powerful than even his fists, Taylor cannot remember the day she became a catalyst, the day Melinda found the dark smudge of bruising on her child's smooth alabaster skin for the first and last time.

(Continued on next page.)

AMBER SCHOLL

"We'll find one with bigger bedrooms. Maybe even a pool." Neither makes mention of the hollowness of such promises, but simply lets them fall into the silent abyss.

The decision to live is not one Melinda will ever live to regret; she will whisk along highways and roll along rocky back roads, soar high over the Earth and navigate turbulent seas before serving another day, another moment, imprisoned. Police, her ex-husband—they can try all they wish to pick up her scent, to drag her back and enclose her in their towering walls, to pry her daughter from her grasp. They have their reasons. But Melinda has a far better one to chase the heels of freedom.

She pulls onto the road, map now spread over her lap and the steering wheel, the road ahead as vast and unknowable as life itself. The rear view mirror paints a two-dimensional portrait, a finite facade that masks the map's incomprehensibly boundless world.

Neither she nor her daughter look back.

Walk With a Mural | Jessica Luebbert

Misery | Sue Wolf

AMBER SCHOLL

Seasons

First blooms of spring,
pollen lightly dusting cars,
stuffy noses, watery eyes,
trapped indoors yet longing,
for the first touch of warmth on the skin,
to be a part of the life reigniting out of reach,
first blistering days of summer,
icy drinks that sweat as we do,
feet burning on black asphalt,
sweltering heat, pool like a refreshing breath,
children laughing, splashing,
enjoying their fleeting freedom,
first colors of fall in the trees,
the muted reds, oranges, yellows,
that top the garish imitations of humans,
light, cool breezes,
winter and summer mingle over us,
with hints of excitement in the wind,
first nips of winter become icy bites,
hot drinks warm the palms of our hands,
slide down our throats to spread throughout,
crackle of the fire, traditions and twinkling lights,
and despite the cold wherever you turn,
pockets of warmth found in subtle places.

AMBER SCHOLL

Journey

The foreseen path drops off into darkness,
smoke clouding the way ahead,
one foot, then another, seeking solid ground,
something to cling to until then,
there is no fleeting kiss goodnight,
no warm embrace or saccharine words,
no patter of tiny scrambling feet,
no nearby white cake and fabric days,
just open seas to drift upon,
a ship to grab a hold of,
at least a wheel to steer from,
a resting place for a single passenger,
a passenger who commits to creativity,
who makes promises to people,
who flirts with exams while dating work,
remains on good terms with evaluative letters,
the ship is alone but never lonely,
the passenger steers, in control,
not of when or where land will appear,
nor of rocky waves, but of the journey itself.

The Nature of Beauty

What is more beautiful,
than nature's complexion,
the stretch of an ocean,
in every direction?
What is more powerful,
than the water's fists,
hammering down,
on all that exists?
What could be more perfect,
than a sky strewn with stars,
sharp curves of the mountains,
rock seared with scars?
But what's lovely is dangerous,
you can't help but spin,
your intricate web,
where we fools meet our ends.

It begins with a breeze,
so light and carefree,
then you are a hurricane,
that destroys all you see.
It begins with a wave,
warm and wet on your feet,
then you are a tidal wave,
that strikes and retreats.
It ends with an asteroid,
a quake of the earth,
inevitable violence,
before the rebirth.
This desire for beauty,
runs so deep in our bones,
Why are we drawn to this?
We're far safer alone.

Things Half-Seen | Debra Crank-Lewis

AMBER SCHOLL

Blind Silence
(To Liz Sheck)

A starless night, a sunless day,
when the world is blinded,
a silent night is not tranquil,
but the result of silenced voices,
behind the wall, scarcely heard,
they whisper, moan, and cry,
mourning creation at its best,
its most natural, honest state.
One, repulsed, sees portraits of shame,
in the pureness of human reflection,
one, repressive, blinds the rest,
bends the world to a whim.
Somewhere along time's twisting line,
bare artificial walls became,
the carelessly comfortable choice,
over nature's bare creation.
The answer never is to blind,
or snatch beauty from the beholder's eye,
from whisper to scream to sweet serenade,
silence is never a choice to be made.

COURTNEY ALLEN

The Quiet

There's a smoke that tries to cover the colors that offer a
perspective different from the monotonous say so of those
who only want us to be surrounded by the gray. It's a pity
when it is ourselves holding the matches. The smog suffocates
the ones who have the most to say but seal their lips shut.
We sit in the corner with a match between our teeth waiting
to strike it so there is no reason to dream. The earth quakes,
begging us to creep from our tents; it should be obvious to tear
up the mountain so we can breathe easy. It's a risky business,
taking the unknown direction while the rest say it is a bad
idea. The climbs and summits may not seem worth the
trouble for some; but to the ones who see the sun winking
behind the smoke, it is a hope. That trail leads somewhere,
even at first when it is in fact nowhere. A journey like that
can seem absurd but that's the point. Those who see that
near invisible speck of reason usually keep it to themselves.

Those matches in our pockets end up dropped into the
river, and when asked where they are we just shrug.
These silent preparations are a strange occurrence to those
who regard us as foolish. We make the trek towards the
nothing-something that tugs at our hearts, and, yes,
some of us will be separated along the way. Some journeys
end in different lands. This is how it is meant to be: The ones
who stay hush and observe what is missing take that first step.

Some snicker that we do nothing except let life pass us by.
They don't realize we're trying everything possible to catch
up to it; we ponder on when to venture on that maiden
voyage. In fact, we're the ones most likely.

Reach | Yvonne Koch

Confident

Leaves curled into crispness
blanket this whole street
while the trees present
their nude selves.
The epitome
of shamelessness.

JULIE E. VARWIG

Jewel-Tipped Trees and a Kiss

Early this morning the trees were wearing jewels.
Now, the setting sun has melted their tips.

I gaze out at them through the window,
Wishing I had someone to touch my lips.

Parched, chapped and cracked;
Would my lips be this way
Had I another pair to moisten them every day?

Perhaps I should let them freeze
as the trees
this morning,
And gleam with the icy jewels they were
adorning.
Would a sunset kiss come then?

Five minutes have passed,
and still,
The trees burn in the sun's light.
How long can a kiss last?
Perhaps someday I'll find out...

Someday, when out through the jewel covered winter,
There's a light and a warmth unlike any other.

My heart will melt
as lips are felt,
And the sunset will disintegrate into
It's own abyss of love.

Giant Washbowl | Kathleen Beardsell

And who knows?
I may remember then
The jewel-tipped trees I see above
Me now.

How long does a sunset kiss last?
The answer:
How can there be a time
When the sun does not shine on a tree?

So someday, that jewel-tipped tree will be me.

Springtime on the Mississippi | Debra Crank-Lewis

JULIE E. VARWIG

As The River

My mind is a frozen river;
My heart:
The current that flows beneath the still, sleek ice.
Ideas fall through the cracks of my mind
To drown in the undertow
Of my willful heart.
For though my mind is as still as the ice,
My heart flows on
As the river.

JULIE E. VARWIG

The Front Yard Lies

Inspired by *"Lafayette Square"*
painting by M. Shawn Cornell in the FAB.

The front yard lies.
Perfect.
Serene.
Not a pink petal out of place.
Not a leaf left lonely.
The home behind it
Must be perfect.
But no.
As surely as the oak tree is structured,
The home is in ruins.
As surely as the roses have bloomed,
The children beneath the roof have failed bud.
And as surely as the fence is sturdy and strong,
The husband and wife crumble day by day.
But what if a front yard has no roses?
And there is no border fence of dignity?
What if there is no blossoming bush or well fed tree?
Would that mean that the greenery reflects the home,
A home tainted with scratched siding and old paint?
No.
For within that house is a family of love.
They have no need for perfect pink roses;
What blooms are the growing hearts of their children.
And what stands sturdy and strong is the resolve of the
husband and wife
Never to let their love whither
As the unfed oak tree in the front yard.

Baby Birds | Kathleen Beardsell

Jake Heels | Sue Wolf

MARY KANE

The Three Wishes

(Inspired by an English folk tale)

"I always get what I ask for"
        he said.
And he smirked.

"Arrogant bastard"
        she said.
And she laughed.
He had three wishes:
He used them carefully.
He wished he'd find
        his life's work.
And he did.
He wished for a woman
who'd love him all his life.
And she did.
And when the shadow fell . . .
and when the shadow fell
It would not do
        to ask to live forever.
"Don't let her grieve for long"
        he said.
And as the time rolled by . . .
and as the time rolled by
She learned to laugh again.

CAMERON BECK

Earthien Sonnet

Oh now but a pale blue dot are you,
In the bleak blackness of cosmic abyss
You have a fiery heart keeping you true,
Until the air breaks and the skies do kiss.
You hang in the dark by just a thin thread
As the patient spider seeks your sphere,
You dip and turn always one step ahead
As he waits for sweet summer to near.
But you are my home on a winter night,
And my mother even when she has passed.
You are my eyes and even so, my might
You are everything you will outlast.
For if I reside in you, you are in me,
That you are, together, all we can be.

Earth | Cameron Beck

CAMERON BECK

Nora the Redeemer

Show me the greenery of day once again.
With the flowers you bring your color to,
That Ra carried through the underworld then
Rose again in deliverance among you.

Show me that the skies are only endless.
And that these clouds are only temporary,
As you follow Apollo and help the world dress
With his fiery horses oh bright fairy!

Show me your effect, but please hide yourself.
My own mortal eyes won't perceive your plight,
As you burn my skin, and hurt my eyes invisible elf,
And give me your life in the form of light!

Show me what you have seen for an eternity.
With Jesus the son, the light as his spirit
We can only wait as you rise with certainty
And reveal the day to those who can't hear it.

Show me your face and its gleaming rays.
As Helios brings the son with golden towers,
To hold all humans in light touch and genuine praise
As you warm their bodies in glittering showers.

The savior of the night, what is your call this morning?
You have a thousand names yet all are so true.
Redeeming each day with your warm forewarning,
Perhaps a word of light, Nora is what I'll call you.

Please show me now, oh Nora the Redeemer.
Your home the sun, and your mirror the moon.
When you leave I wonder at night, a dreamer,
But I am not scared — for you will, come again soon.

EMILY McGUIRE

Astronomy

Looking up at the stars
Watching the waves come in and out
Mending a broken heart
Knowing this is just the start
Feeling the cool sand between his toes
Wondering if it had all been just a show.

Alex | Sue Wolf

Blooming Vibrance | Erin Petty

TYRA BOWMAN

Fleur

If all the world were flowers
let me not be a daisy or a rose.
Daisies are picked apart
as if they can somehow decide our fate.
Roses are kind of cliché
and frankly overrated.
Let me be a dandelion,
for even when I'm uprooted
the parts of me can create new life.

TYRA BOWMAN

Mulatto

When she was four,
she didn't realize she was different.
She was raised by grandparents who
never drew attention to the fact she was
golden brown like the sand in her sandbox
and not milky white like the rest of her family.
When she was ten,
she hated that she looked different.
Her classmates pointed out that
her hair was kinky and nappy and
her skin was sometimes ashen like a bonfire log.
When she was fifteen,
she started to grow into her different.
A new school, a fresh start brought
kinder peers; ones who were curious.
She started to blossom into the kind of person she wanted
to be.
When she was nineteen,
she finally realized that
it wasn't her appearance that made her different,
it was the fact that she saw not the color of people's skin,
she saw the color of their hearts.

SABRINA TEEPLE

Cannibal

i think about your fingers tracing the inside of my heart
(i am bleeding because i squeezed your hand)
i think about your laugh piercing through my soul
(i am nothing but holes because i pulled away)
i think about your face indenting my mind
(i am blind because i looked at another)
i think about your lips eating at my mind
(i am thoughtless because i wouldn't let you taste me)

In The Basement | Sabrina Teeple

SABRINA TEEPLE

DIY Psych

when i fall apart in the darkness
you put me back together with hairspray
when i am pale from this sickness
you brighten me with lipstick prints
when i think it's time to go
you keep me here with your pantyhose
when i want to drink myself to sleep
you intoxicate me with your black dress
when i am without you i remember
your hairspray
your lipstick
your pantyhose
your black dress
and just from the thought of you
i am together
i am bright
i am here
i am intoxicated

MEGAN ZEHNDER

Ode to a Tree

Oh, Seed, your capsule conceals you.
A delicate embryo, you dwell, immersed,
in the cavity of the Earth's womb.
With every breath, moisture pierces through your
skeleton, germinating your cells; emerging your leaves.
Oh, Seed, how you tantalize threads of air, soaring,
they vigorously penetrate the soil—fervent to stimulate
your sprouting.
Oh, Sapling, your seedlings bore from the fetus of your
shell. Even in infancy your leaves cusped the skin of the
Earth's belly burrowing through the dirt; straining for the
first caress of sunlight.
Your roots delved, integrating among the tissues of the
ground. Foraging past clay and rock, you Sapling, clasped
your limbs to the heart of the Earth, embracing your
creator; your mother.
With a craving to cultivate, your feeble stem
flourished in the breeze; fumbling to grasp warmth.
With each droplet of rain your leaves drank in the water;
thriving.
With every inhalation of carbon dioxide your trunk seeped
oxygen.
Oh, Tree, your buds blossom to the scent of Spring.
Your branches extend beyond the sight of man. Your shaft
captures the rings of age; revealing your immortality.
Oh, Tree, you shade the humanity of nature. You Tree,
immense and firm, reign against the punitive winter,
housing the homeless and the frail.
With each season, you mature; relinquishing your leaves
to the Autumn wind, only to fully flower at the vestige of
Summer.

Blowing in the Wind | Crystal Ianelli

Oh, Tree, you, too, shall conceive a child, which will impregnate the womb of the Earth, prosper in its belly and breach its skin to prevail forever, with worth; just as you have done.

Hanging on the Line | Kayla Czajkowski

MEGAN ZEHNDER

The Wife

Shades of soft indigo, silver, and mauve flooded the house.
Unfamiliar china was displayed on the dining table.
A tinfoil hat was positioned at the head seat.
The scent of cinnamon lingered in the air. An echoing of
delicate notes resonated, furnishing every vacant room.
The wife hummed an earworm melody she heard on the radio.
She checked the oven. The browning muffin top of the cake
crowned its facade above the pan.
The wife caught a glimpse of herself in the mirror.
Her eyes glistened and her cheeks were flushed.
Brain candy.
The timepiece for the cake chimed.
As she reached for the pan the phone rang.
"Hello?" The wife's lips dwindled into sorrow.
"You're working late, again?" The woman whimpered
a weak laugh.
"No, it's alright."

MIRIAM HANNIBAL

Cast

B e forewarned, the step's not there,
R eady your nerves, you're in for a scare.
O ne little misjudgment is all it takes, and
K RASH! BANG! BOOM!
E very bone will feel the quakes.
N ow you're laying on an old steel bed,
A nticipating the painkiller to spread.
N ervous anxiety provokes your fears,
K indling up a flooding stream of tears.
L ike a bat out of hell you stumble and fight,
E nduring it all with crutches held tight.

My Last Lullaby

I sat there, holding you in my arms,
Staring down into your soft, pink face,
And the thought of giving you to them forever,
Made me cry harder than ever.
I sat there holding you, wondering,
If the adoptive parents knew what I was doing;
The sacrifice we were both giving them,
My sacrifice of relinquishing my most precious gem.
I stood up, holding you tightly,
And all I could do was sing for you,
Through glistening tears and a closed throat.
I sang my last lullaby, every last note.
I walked to the door, holding my heart in my arms
While the sobs threatened to reappear.
I held them back as I opened the gate to your future,
Closing down our 9-month special feature.

Little Lamb | Kayla Czajkowski

I sit here now, holding your picture close
Smiling down at you in tears with a closed throat.
They honored our sacrifice and left me with a promise,
That they would raise you well, provide me with solace:
I was not to be forgotten.
That you would be spoiled rotten.
There would never be a bit of drama.
And you'd grow up knowing I was your First Mama.

JORDAN STARKEY

Serenade Betrayed

Within a private orchard on the page,
Behind a wall divorced from act and scene,
Of lyric lines a balcony as stage
Composed awaits beneath a deep serene;
Therein the music of the lark is still,
The moon is constant and the earth at rest,
And in a dreamless slumber lies the will
Beside adventure, story, deed, and gest;
As I and my true verse in whispers purled,
In eddied kisses and in circling arms,
So whirl from out the currents of the world
To drown within an idle pool of charms;
Till floating up we drain into the street
Of drama's passing hour, noise, and heat.
A Pair of Star-Crossed Lovers.

Dignity Digested

How edible am I from feet to chops,
The Diet of Worms
A feast of unmatched form and flesh august,
A menu of most admirable slops,
A dish whose crust is quintessential dust;
Whose noble mind, or boiled or baked or stewed,
Or served as a ragout or fricassee,
Is too a wholesome, nourishing brain food
Without a gram of fat or calorie;
Whose part most yummy yet and true dessert,
A dainty certes to die for sans compare,

Potted Meat | Given Zane

Brand: **Armour**
Type: **Potted Meat**

INGREDIENTS: Mechanically Separated Chicken, Partially Defatted Pork Fatty Tissue (Tocopherol, Natural Flavor, and Citric Acid), Water, Salt, Contains 2% Or Less Of: Mustard, Vinegar, Dextrose, Sodium Erythorbate, Garlic Powder, Natural Flavors, Sodium Nitrate.

Less than a dollop or a dash of dirt-
The import of my life as light as air;
Though crammed on consequence and fatted full,
I fated am to be a brunch of bull.

LINDSAY BRAND

Cerulean Blue Period

Swirling around in my cup, the rich brown coffee
collides with the cream sending rippling waves against
the handmade cerulean blue cup. I tell my friends, I say,
it's the simple pleasures of life that really make life
meaningful and shit. Then they tell me to get a job
in an office.

Look over that at those ancient brick buildings wrapped
in the blue blanket of the sky. Offices are cold, unfeeling
metal papoose wrappings. I sip the mud brown coffee
again letting its caffeinated muscle invigorate my tired
soul. Someone somewhere should write this down.
That's some great wordplay.

My knapsack hanging by one strap on the back of the
bistro chair is home to a moleskin notebook, pens, gum
wrappers, and band flyers. Repurposed fashion, it is made
of an old postal bag. I wish I had met that worker, but
remnants of his soul remain. My bag is like dog catnip.

Man with baseball hat walks by. Teenager sagging his
pants walks the opposite way. Going to board with his
friends, little tagger. There's a middle-aged woman with
too much lipstick and flared jeans.

I wish I could meet someone. A nice girl. She will be
fascinating like me, and like nature. Find joy in the simple
things. Tattoos are good.

On Rabbits

Dodging around in my backyard – lives a small gray rabbit.
Christened Horace Van Buren, he is a gentleman in waiting.
He nods at the dogs housed next door.

He inspects my garden's produce,
finding it wanting. Then I found a nest of baby bunnies in
the long, un-mowed grass. I guess that means he is a lady.

Track Star | Russell Ward

Found My Marbles | Hannah Clark

DIANA NASH

Junk

Jammed deep inside my brain,
There is a junk drawer,
Where idle thoughts,
And long forgotten memories reside.
Seldom opened, crammed with
Mental rubber bands,
Paperclips, staples,
Discarded connectors, without content.
A, double A, triple A
C, and D batteries,
Tiny round ones
For grandma's hearing aid, lost years ago.
Pens and pencils roll
From side to side
Aimlessly, without
Ink or lead or a person to hold them.

Mismatched receipts and tags
Wrinkled, faded, thin
Paper with nonsensical digits
Kept just in case things didn't work out.
I dare not open this drawer
Revealing my odds and ends.
Erasing their magical protection.
Exposing their truth.
Traumatic scraps,
Shoved in the drawer,
Subconsciously filed remnants
No dates, no names, no context.
A collage of a shiny coins, red crayon,
Matchbooks, loose screws,
Sharp pins and a black and white photo,
Blue waves and white sand.

DIANA NASH

NCLB

Mandated educational concern:
Why is this boy failing?
Test him
Find the reason he is not proficient.
      Analyze the data.
      Send a new teacher.
      Where are his weaknesses?
      Write an Individual Leaning Plan
      Put the boy in special classes
      Fire the instructors.
      Replace the administrators.
      Someone make him a capable student.
Mandated social concern:
Why is this boy failing?
Human, compassionate response:
Feed him
Find the reason he is not at school.
      Analyze the community.
      Make his home safe.
      Heal his body.
      Give him a role model.
      Show the boy that he is important
      Surround him with moral behavior
      Employ his parents
      Dignify his existence.
Mandated community concern:
Why don't you care about this boy?
      Beyond legislation
      Beyond classroom walls
      Beyond the privileged perspective.

Personal teacher concern:

     How can one profession save the world?

     Where is the money?

     Where are the parents?

     What about this kid's reality?

Boys like this boy live in our cities

     in our small towns

        in our suburbs.

They walk our streets, attend our schools,

and sleep in our homes.

These boys are white, black, brown, biracial . . .

They are the outcast sons of America

Floating down the river of denial.

Analyze the data.

     This boy is not important.

     There is money, but not for his rescue.

     His personal life is tragic.

     His future? Statistically predictable.

Parental concern.

     What about my boy?

     Who's gonna protect my boy,

     From the thugs, the gangs, the drugs, the guns?

     Ain't no safe place, even for a good boy.

Government concern.

     Reduce entitlements

     Keep good Americans safe

     Close failing schools

     Build more prisons

     Bury our mistakes.

SHAMGAUD SHUTTLESWORTH

Military Poetrie

My day starts as it ends,
With prayer...thanks and request for forgiveness...
asking God to bless my buddy to the left of me,
my gear, and my weaponry.
That my shot is straight, my judgement unclouded,
And no bomb goes unfounded, now we may proceed.
Same war new country, priorities changed,
bring the soldiers under my command home,
allowed 30 minutes max on the phone
loved ones raising your young alone.
Put that to the back of your mind
climbing up the side of your armored ride
you've no time to be distracted,
showing a presence as you travel the roads trying to rid
Afghanistan of Taliban one city at a time starting with
Jalalabad.
Violence, radio silence, language barriers,
all odds stacked against us,
some of the elders have massive walls of mistrust
Discuss the disgust of American people.
Sharing promises and ideas over tea
or... plotting attacks against us disguised as police.
Dodging mortars, rockets,and the deceitful,
Fighting for those decent, prosperous, and peaceful,
Marching through villages on dismounted patrols listening
to chants, raves, rants and such...children smiling as they
run by with their fist high and both thumbs up.
My fist filled with pride held to the sky as the other
squeezes an M4 tightly slightly wishing a sucka would
make like a customer and try me.

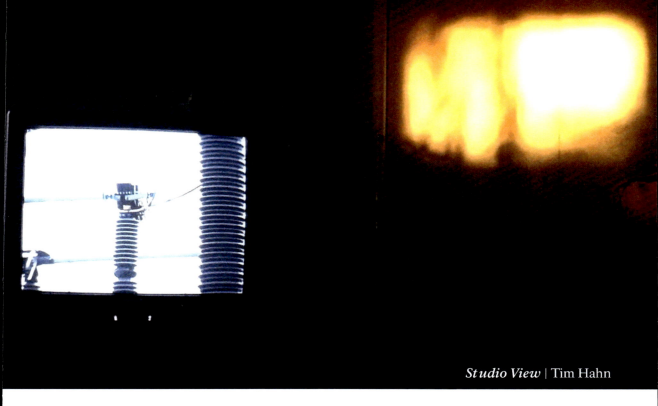

Studio View | Tim Hahn

Under the watchful eye of the enemy from the
surrounding 347 degrees of mountain tops we fight,
shots penetrate deep inside the sandbags in front of me,
I fire back take that you evil person I can't see.
Hot Gatorade quenches me,
cold cuts with no luck for cooked lunch we suffer,
Pushing forward with the intent of intense,
Still amazed a military discount is only 10%,
Yet we are far and few not all can do what we do.
I challenge you to stomp rocks in my boots,
Quake sands in distant lands,
Put your life at risk for no extra money,
I challenge you to sign the contract once
cause I signed 3 times and gonna be a fourth,
enjoy your safety that we fight for.

Lobby Boxer | Warren Rich

MARY HORNER

Cacophony

Beneath the stringy facts
Lies the space where
Beautiful ugly twists itself Into a hole
Like music from the night fills my ear,
Fighting for space in a predetermined
Battle of sounds, and you think you can
Divide it into separate memories,
But it goes to the same place
With the garbage truck,
The wailing baby, and
Whispers against you.
The only hopes we have fall
Under the heading of interpretation
Or false memories,
Both of which may
Fail us within a week, maybe two.

MARY HORNER

Memory Lame

When I open the door
To a place I've been,
Will I recognize it as
Either too close
Or too far, in a strange
Moment of nothing
Where it should be?
The starting point follows
A path of yesterdays
That no longer exists,
Where words turn into
Night and day,
Man and woman
Fork and knife.

Parallelism | Henry Salazar

KASEY PERKINS

The Metatarsal Galaxy

I see the stars
on your foot—
the metatarsal galaxy,
a milky
way, milky
skin with thin
ions of ink
sprouting like bones,
antitails to
phalanges.

I know machines
once slipped
the tips
of needles, medial
points of light like
a telescope
through the night
through your skin—

blood and blue
as various hues in space
sweeping swaths
comet-like
over flesh, a liquid
nebula
a shower
of tattooed meteors.

KASEY PERKINS

Mississippi Night

Within this bliss which
mimics his hips, his
illicit lips (slick with
gilding tints) I—
bridging schism in
twisting midnight, in
timid highlights, in
limpid lightning—
sift insipid silt, lilt
within his igniting iris,
sighing, shining:
gifting risk which splits,
splicing this ibis
nightlight.

Inheritance

I have placed your clothes in the dumpster
outside the university, longed to commit sati

with your journals, wishing to throw myself
upon the pyre like a wife married to

her love's life work—and here
I find your gold hamsa earrings buried between

the carpet and the wall, two gold
hands, their inner eyes wide as I untangle

them from the shimmering Berber
and push them through my own ears,

piercing my lobes with the thought of yours,
the same metal through different flesh—

these ten golden fingers wrapped up with mine,
warding away evil eyes, bad luck.

KASEY PERKINS

The First Storm of February

A jolt in the muscle—
I slowly become
awake,
eyes sealed and unrevealed,
yet still pulling my heavy, sodden mind
soaked from the pool
of sleep
onto land, and
the roar of my snores fades
into the early morning thunder.

I like this role I play—
my heart, a school bell
in my chest.

I think about spring
and whether
or not it still exists.

Deer Creek | Kayla Czajkowski

Winter's Perch | Kayla Czajkowski

KIM LEE SEAGULL

The Canadian Snowbird

In a careful methodical way
In order to protect or to shield his people
From the manic rage of a Golden Eagle
The anxious Cherokee Eagle Slayer
Upon his great return to the Tribe
Wisely proclaimed that he had killed
A Snowbird and not an Eagle
The tiny Snowbird being too insignificant
To be dreaded by his people.

HALEY McGROTTY

The First Time

Everyone should remember their first time.
The first time is supposed to be special.
You're not supposed to regret it.
I wish I could wash it all away
Like the rain washes away the dirt
on the streets before the storm.

Idea of Peace in a Fish Tank | Julie Westrich

Mourier | Kathleen Beardsell

AMBER DUNLAP

The Mausoleum

The old mausoleum was cracked straight down the middle
like some god in his anger had shot a bolt of lightning at it.
The granite walls were choked with ivy; the Corinthian columns
were positively strangled with it.
The air around the mausoleum tasted heavily of lilac, like bitterness
and regret. Every time the doors to the mausoleum creaked open on nearly
broken hinges it produced a sort of sinking feeling in your stomach.
There was no real reason for feeling this way except for the sound conjured
images of bony fingers reaching from beyond the veil of death for you.
I used to think that was why people died—because the door to the world
of death had opened like Pandora's Box. In my mind, Death waited patiently
just on the other side of that door for some idiot to open it. Once out in the
world he would steal lives in a flash so that he could return before the
doors closed again. The doors don't open anymore. The ivy had grown so thick
that only bits and pieces of the granite are visible. Some days I think
that is enough to hold Death back. Other days I see the funeral processions
passing by and remember that there are other doorways to Hell.

CONTRIBUTORS

Courtney Allen
I was never good at sports, that is until I started participating in this blood sport called writing. At twenty two you'd think I'd learn to where a helmet by now.

Kathleen Beardsell
Kathleen Beardsell is a nature enthusiast who is interested in electronic literature, open source initiatives, digital culture, and technology. She teaches writing at St Charles Community College and St Louis Community College-Wildwood and holds an MFA from Brown University.

Cameron Beck
Cameron Beck is a growing father, son, student, writer, musician, and manager. A young man from Saint Peters, Cameron is looking to see the rest. He writes music and poetry and is pursuing studies in English and literature while building a family.

Tyra Bowman
Tyra Bowman is a empowered and creative writer and photographer who enjoys exploring and finding inspiration in her everyday surroundings.

Lindsay Brand
Lindsay Brand lives in St. Charles, Missouri and teaches English. In her spare time, she enjoys reading, eating mint chocolate chip ice cream, and secretly being an optimist. She has published previously in *The Monarch Review*.

Debra Crank-Lewis
Debra Crank-Lewis grew up on a farm surrounded by a wonderful extended family. There are many teachers in her family tree so perhaps her calling was set early on. She has two WONDERFUL children. Reading, travel, cooking, storytelling and now, perhaps photography are among her interests.

Kayla Czajkowski
Kayla Czajkowski was born, raised, and currently resides in St. Louis, Missouri. Photography has always been a source of great interest and pleasure to her. She loves spending time enjoying the simplistic beauty of the country, particularly with her camera. Kayla hopes to continue her photographic pursuits throughout her life.

Dana Delibovi

Dana Delibovi's work has appeared in *The Formalist, Anderbo.com, Orphic Lute, Mid Rivers Review, Spirituality and Health, Red Tape, and The Poetry Society's Poetry in Motion Series*. She is an associate editor at *Boulevard Magazine* in St. Louis. She is also an adjunct professor of Philosophy at Lindenwood University. Dana was recently selected as a 30/30 project poet at Tupelo Press.

Amber Dunlap

Amber Dunlap used to spend her summers up in Lamont with her grandma and grandpa. They used to live just down the road from the old Lamont Cemetery, and her brothers and she enjoyed sneaking out there and telling ghost stories. The place stuck with her.

Kristen Garcia

Kristen Garcia spends most of her day writing, drawing, playing games, and crying over television. When not doing these things, she can typically be found at work making funeral programs. She enjoys good books, well cooked meals, and fluffy cats.

Lacey Garland

Lacey Garland is a writing enthusiast. She graduated in May, and she enjoyed school the most when she was in English or writing classes.

Tim Hahn

Tim Hahn BFA from the Kansas City Art Institute. MFA Washington University. Adjunct at SCC for 25 years.

Harleigh Heck

Harleigh Heck tries not to live a life that she would not be proud to look back upon. She realizes that life is not refreshing and invigorating; it is rough and raw and uncomfortable. However, she makes life comfortable through meager means.

CONTRIBUTORS

Mary Horner

Mary Horner is the author of *Strengthen Your Nonfiction* and blogs at writRteachr.blogspot.com. She is the former managing editor of the *Journal of the American Optometric Association* and earned writing/editing certification from the American Medical Writers Association. She earned her writing certificate from the University of Missouri St. Louis. She teaches communications at St. Louis and St. Charles Community Colleges.

Crystal Iannelli

Crystal Iannelli is a mover, traveler, photographer, teacher, faithful lover. What wakes her up in the morning is to watch her preschoolers use their creative minds and imaginations.

Mary Kane

Mary Kane is an expatriate of suburban Chicago. A lifelong learner with a passion for poetry, she lives in St. Charles and attends St. Charles Community College. She is a frequent contributor to *Mid Rivers Review*.

Daron Kappauff

Daron Kappauff is a father, a husband, a storyteller, and a poet. He is also an adjunct professor of English and an aspiring novelist and comic book writer.

Yvonne S. Koch

When Yvonne S. Koch is not teaching or enjoying time with her family she loves to travel and spend time outdoors. Her appreciation of God's nature draws her to creating landscape photography. More of her photography may be viewed at www.Behance.net/YKoch.

Jessica Luebbert

Jessica Luebbert is a photographer who can be found on an adventure at any given time, talks to animals about as much as people, and always laughs more than breathes. She also finds passion in composing quirky blog posts that are more distracting than informing.

Haley McGrotty

Haley McGrotty is nineteen years old and a student at St. Charles Community College. She loves to express how she feels through writing and dancing. She has been dancing since she was three years old. She plans to become a special needs teacher at the elementary level and continue to pursue her love for poetry and writing.

Emily McGuire

Emily McGuire is a 23-year-old student at St..Charles Community College studying sociology and psychology.

Alison Ouellette-Kirby

Alison Ouellette-Kirby is an artist and has been a faculty member at St. Charles Community College since 1999.

Diana Nash

Diana Nash has taught speech, drama, and English for over 30 years. She started teaching in Thailand, but has spent the rest of her career in St. Charles County. In her free time, she has raised two sons and a daughter. A sign in her kitchen reads, "Grandchildren are the reward for not strangling your teenagers."

Hali Pace

Hali Pace is nineteen years old. She has six brothers and sisters. She is an English major. When she graduates, she wants to work as a publisher. When she retires, she hopes to own a bookstore.

Lauren Pearson

Lauren Pearson would like her writing to give someone the inspiration to live their life with the understanding that pain, fear, and confusion are as integral to being whole as happiness, love, and contentment.

CONTRIBUTORS

Kasey Perkins
Kasey Perkins is a teacher, editor, and writer who completed her MFA in poetry at the University of Missouri St. Louis. She is the recipient of the 2014 Margaret Leong Children's Poetry Prize, and her poems have appeared in the *Wisconsin Review*.

Erin Petty
Erin Petty lives in St. Charles, Missouri, where she was born and raised. She recently received her Associates of Arts degree from St. Charles Community College, and plans to continue her education at the University of Missouri – Columbia, majoring in environmental sciences. Her photographic work, which includes landscapes, as well as flora and fauna, is heavily influenced by her lifelong love of nature and the environment.

Warren Rich
Warren Rich is President, CEO of several companies in the automotive and trucking industry. Retired in 2003, he expanded a lifelong interest in photography to more than a hobby. He enjoys street photography, both people and scenes., and he specially like the challenges of photographing his grandchildren and their activities. He believes that if his images give the viewers pleasure, then all the better.

Henry Salazar
Henry Salazar is always willing to adventure and keep it real. EHarmony and twerking never fail to crack him up. TYBG.

Sarah Salveggio
Sarah Salveggio graduated from St. Charles Community College in 2013. She plans on going back to finish up a bachelor's degree shortly after returning from a year long working holiday in New Zealand.

Amber Scholl
Amber Scholl is a recent graduate of St. Charles Community College. Besides writing, her other hobbies include reading, crocheting, and trying out craft ideas from Pinterest. She enjoys spending time with her family, friends, and pets.

Kim Lee Seagull

Kim Lee Seagull always prays before he writes, for after all, poetry is holy and the reason for its success is not an earthly, but a transcendental one, since it comes from the invisible world.

Shamgaud Shuttlesworth

Shamgaud Shuttlesworth was born and raised in Chicago, Illinois and currently serves in the United States Army with 226th MWD detachment out of Fort Hood, Texas. He has been serving in the military for twelve years.

Brian D. Smith

Brian D. Smith is currently a professor in the Visual Art department at St. Charles Community College. His artwork has been exhibited nationally and is held in numerous public and private collections. He is represented by the Duane Reed Gallery in St. Louis, Missouri.

Jordan Starkey

Jordan Starkey continues to rapidly decay towards death; he nevertheless remains optimistically deluded.

April Stout

April Stout created the "Castles in the Sky" body of work to honor and encourage the artistic endeavors of her 4 children. She is the owner of Sweet Effects photography, now based in Pinehurst, NC. She does commercial panoramic photography as a Google Trusted Agency Photographer, in addition to wedding, family and portrait work.

Sabrina Teeple

Sabrina Teeple isn't sure about much anymore.

Julie Varwig

Julie Varwig is a college student studying English at St. Charles Community College. Though young, she has been writing poetry for more than a decade and has begun to dabble her pen in fiction and blogging. Julie hopes to teach English Literature in the future, as well as English as a Second Language.

CONTRIBUTORS

Russell Ward
Russell Ward has made it into his mid-twenties. He runs on no sleep and Amp energy drinks in order to take care of his family. He spends as much time in the wilderness as he possibly can. He associates with questionable characters. "I have a good life," he said.

Sara Welch
Sara Welch is a young, though, maturing author, who believes wholeheartedly in the power of words, honesty and espresso. Overwhelmingly appreciative and elated to have been given a corner to call home in the *Mid River Review*, she is hopeful that this will not be her last appearance.

Julie Westrich
Julie Westrich is not the loudest person around and it's always been easier to show someone what she's about than tell them. That's why she started and continues to take photos, to explain things to herself and to other people.

Sue Wolf
Sue Wolf is a St. Louis native and St. Peters resident. She singles out her daughters for being her greatest joy in life. They have been strong supporters of their mother's photography, often helping to critique her work.

Given Zane
Given Zane is a 21-year-old photographer based out of the Saint Louis Missouri area. He's currently going to college for Software Engineering with a minor in photography. He's been taking photographs seriously for over a decade now and has no intention of stopping any time soon.

Megan Zehnder
Megan Zehnder graduated from St. Charles Community College this year.
She adores writing and has loved being involved in classes in the English department.
She has found inspiration and enjoyment from her time at St. Charles Community College.